How Not to Choose Peace

Vedanth.K

Imagination encircles the world

Preface

It is with great joy and a sense of accomplishment that I present this anthology to my esteemed readers.

This narrative explores an alternative reality of the world during the Nazi rule over Germany, and how the downfall during WWII gave birth to a large form of democracy.

I hope this what-if fiction, sparks your imagination, evokes emotions, and leaves a lasting mark on your literary journey. Thank you for choosing the book.

Cheers

Introduction

How Not to Choose Peace is a what-if fiction, based in Nazi Germany during the course of WWII. The writing is set in a utopian Nazi-led Europe, which primarily explores an alternate reality on how Hitler rose to power, and how his subsequent downfall moulded a flourishing democracy. The narrative is a blend of reality and added fiction. Have fun flying through a Nazi-led paradise!

How Not to Choose Peace is a what-if fiction, based in Nazi Germany during the course of WWII. The writing is set in a utopian Nazi-led Europe, which primarily explores an alternate reality on how Hitler rose to power, and how his subsequent downfall moulded a flourishing democracy. The narrative is a blend of reality and added fiction. Have fun flying through a Nazi-led paradise!

How Not to Choose Peace

Prologue

The engine:

The conclusion of WW1 came about with the Allies arranging for Germany, the most imposing of treaties as a farewell - The Versailles Treaty. The farewell was mean, yet generous and humble, for it gifted Germany with grand reparations and a little too much humiliation.

The terms of the treaty were so harsh that it outraged and disturbed the true patriots of the black-red-gold. Among them, was yet another wounded veteran of the First World War named Adolf Hitler, largely unknown and politically naive or at least as of then...

Adolf Hitler was humiliated by the unjust defeat of Germany, or more seemingly the undeserved victory of the Allied forces in the war. He reasoned that the loss was due to the actions of patriotic traitors within the Weimar, whom he started regarding as inferiors - a notion that hence fuelled his political passion.

The German Workers' Party worked on similar political ideas as Hitler did. But the party lacked serious representation and coordination. To capitalise on this opportunity, he joined the party, where he progressively built and inculcated his ideas, garnered trust, propelled his rank, and ultimately took over the party and renamed it 'The Nazi Party'.

He changed the party symbol to the Swastika, a symbol that turned from being an association of religious divinity to a symbol that would then take to terrorise millions. Hitler was ideological in the selection of Swastika, as he believed Swastika had been and will hence eternally be a representation of anti-semitic ideas. And so would it, forever changing the connotation of 'Swastika'!

Yet, his anti-semitic ideas arose not randomly, not by intention, nor by force, but just as a natural acquaintance of dislike from his political likes, within the country and out.

The fuel:

Hitler never invented Jewish hatred as history says. But he did really patent that idea, which had existed for a long time. Jews endorsed communism - the ideology that almost all Western leaders had discouraged for ages. And so did Adolf Hitler! Communism was hated, and so were the Jews!

The fuel for Hitler's political engine was his hatred towards Jewish ideology, and not Jews themselves.

The discussion of the Nazi reign would be incomplete and unjust without comprehending the other dimension of truth - the conspired political plans of the Jews, aimed at world dominance!

There had been strong conspiracy theories from the days of Spartacus-Weishaupt to those of Karl Marx and Trotsky and then down to Adolf Hitler, alleging that the Jews had been endorsing communist principles and that they were working to achieve world domination. The idea of Jewish-Bolshevism and ZOG (Zionist-occupied government), claimed that the Jews already hold passive control over the politics of Western governments, and were working to soon take over world politics.

Post the first world war, the speculations about Jewish Bolshevism and Zionist principles took light and became a subject of interest among the Western governments, as it seemed like these strong conspiracy subjects were stronger than conceived of.

So, countries feared they might fall victim to the Jewish spell, and that Jews may pose a threat to their political future...

As they feared, the successful Bolshevik revolution in Russia which overthrew the government, terrorised the political world.

Everyone feared. The mightiest of the European powers feared. The strongest of the political heads feared. Even those with forces and arms feared. The revolution created a vibration globally. Not for it was nuclear, not for it was despotic, not for it was anti-human, but only owing to the reason that it was Jewish-led!

By then, the perception that communism and Bolshevism were Jewish-inspired had become a theory that was impossible to neglect. Under Hitler, that theory had become more solid and officialised.

The failure of Germany in the First World War, despite its highly capable armed forces, was blamed on the Jewish traitors within the country. During the war, most of the important positions in the Republic were Jewish represented. These leaders worked against German interests, and the lack of necessary actions during the war justified and validated the conspiracy theories in a way.

These recurring Jewish actions, starting with the Bolshevik revolution in Russia, followed by the betrayal in Germany infuriated Hitler.

Adolf Hitler, who earlier was rather Philo-Semitic, slowly transitioned to an anti-semite.

Anti-semitism was already a pre-established idea in Western political culture, and as any political representative did, and would, Hitler acknowledged and acquainted himself with the same idea.

Nothing to blame on Hitler, indeed.

The theory that the Jews intoxicate the political space had him convinced that the Jewish community must first be cleansed in order to pursue his political ambitions. Not only did Hitler hold this notion. Churchill did, Stalin did, Roosevelt did, and even Mussolini did, but no one was discredited to the scale Hitler was - for no one else had the solid courage to assert those ideas publicly as Hitler had.

By blaming the Jews for Western political instability, Hitler created a stereotypical enemy and hence worked to expel them - which in time grew into a racist outlook.

So, anti-semitism and Jewish hatred were in culture for ages, but the only person who took to capitalising on those ideas was Hitler - which if it hadn't happened would have wrought out a Jewish-led communist world.

The run:

In just a few years of holding power, Hitler, through his witty tactics built for himself the political environment he had long yearned to mould, and slowly started raising ranks from there. He began to align his plans in the line to assure a pure political space and to eliminate all those traitors whom he found undesirable in his political script.

Adolf Hitler organised public speeches and rallies, which he believed were a fluent medium to propagate Nazi ideologies to the people, and that, it would aid him in establishing the idea of 'his people 'rather than 'the people'.

This would go on for years, slower, yet surer!

A few years into the Nazi rule, Hitler, having convinced 'his' people of the Nazi ideologies and having achieved what he had sought to craft with his utterly spellbinding voice, realised that everything was then internally stable.

So, Hitler set out to further his ambitious, yet terrorising plans to take over Europe!

He carefully sensed the Western geopolitical instability and started scripting plans to wrap his fist around the European countries. Hitler, along with his ministers, implicitly drafted a series of attacks that would expand the reach of Swastika and establish their dream of 'A Thousand Year Reich'.

According to the plan, they would initially set out slowly, capturing the lands they had lost during the First World War. Then, they would target the Western European powers - which would help forge a solid military backing. And finally, they would move on to take over the East - which Hitler hoped would serve as the 'living space' - as he termed it - for 'his' people.

Hitler always felt a sense of humiliation when reminded of the Versailles treaty - which indeed had fuelled his political charisma so far. According to the treaty, Germany wouldn t be sanctioned to construct land, air or naval forces and the country wouldn t be a centre for military developments. Hitler, being a man of words, strictly abided by the same - indeed! He began expanding his infantry, equipping them, and organising sounding rallies to project his sturdily trained Nazi muscles to the Allies, who had served him the nice treat(y).

Having shaped a highly puissant infantry, he went on to build a military backing to aid hem. The Nazi Air Force - Luftwaffe, the Navi -

Kriegsmarine, and the land forces - Wehrmacht. All set to carry Hitler s ideals to the world!

The military development in Germany unsurprisingly sparked interest globally, and as natural as the situation seemed, countries anticipated a forthcoming war - one that would surely rewrite geopolitics. And, they were right!

1

The Inauguration

Kicking into gear, the Nazis' tackle began with an unprovoked attack on the Polish soil. The first shot was grandly fired into the borders, officially inaugurating the Second World War!

Within hours of the invasion, the Wehrmacht commenced their aggression, devastating everything in sight, staining the soil with blood and bullets, while the Luftwaffe was swishing overhead. Polish towns were shelled intensely, destroying establishments and wiping away men.

Despite the dominance of Nazi troops on the field, the Polish military made their best efforts to control the German command, as they had better position inland than Germany did.

However, having a mere position without compatible forces exhausted the Polish military. In a few days, the Wehrmacht took control over major cities and air bases. Further, communication channels were disrupted to detour the Polish troops.

The Polish military was no match for Hitler's war machine, as the German forces were dominant and overpowered.

The Nazi infantry easily broke into the Polish defences and swept away the unarmed Poles. The innocent Poles were left with nowhere to go but either died protesting or agreed to concede with German demands.

Soon, in an attempt to bring a part of the land under German control, Warsaw was bombarded. The last resistance of the Polish units ended, and Western Poland was taken control of. With it, Hitler boldly asserted what was to come for the future!

The Poles, being slow in mobilising troops, fell victim to the Nazis' 'Blitzkrieg'.

Following this disaster in the west, the Russians began their hunt in the east - in accordance with the secret protocol of the non-aggression pact - soon demoting the Polish government to the point of a gun and forcing their surrender.

A stench of burning and a grey veil of smoke covered the entirety of Poland.

Britain and France came to the understanding that appeasement was no longer a viable approach to stopping Hitler's war machine. And as promised, Britain and France stood by their guarantee of Poland's borders and declared war against Nazi Germany.

The Polish invasion served as an experiment and demonstration of the 'Blitzkrieg' war tactic, developed by Hitler's young Nazi associate known by the alias "AthenH."

He was the most trusted Nazi fellow and shared a remarkably close relationship with Adolf Hitler. Despite being the youngest Nazi leader, he was appointed head of the ministry for his exceptional war-planning skills...

AthenH had been shaping the Blitzkrieg strategy all along the way while Adolf Hitler was busy with his propaganda models in the early years. He had garnered unwavering trust among the Nazi delegates and had instilled a strong conviction in them about his abilities, and thus held a fairly respectable position among the other high-profile Nazis.

It was always hard to persuade the entrenched Nazi order to shift from Hitler's intuitive beliefs, which could be achieved only through skilled flattery. And AthenH of course, did thread the needle, tailoring his flattery to the very sentiments of Hitler and rerouting the Nazi ideals to align with his own political plans that he had secretly been working upon!

Now that 'Blitzkrieg' worked well on Polish soil, it would be hence enforced for future European conquests and other further expansions on the horizon.

Hitler was now all set to tackle his foes - France and Britain with the solid army that he had moulded through the years.

2

The Hitback

With the war declared, Germany first eyed France over Britain.

Hitler aimed at a full investment of troops directly into the borders, seeking a swift victory. He rapidly assembled as many land forces as his military could feed and prepared for battle.

Nevertheless, AthenH posed rather a contrasting, yet fair plan to wrap up France even quicker. He understood the instability of the existing political order in France, which would hence retard the coordination of the forces on the field. The unstable democracy would also hinder the military from acting independently and immediately, thereby limiting their capability to respond to the Nazi surprises. Leveraging the enemy's inability to quickly command both land and aerial assaults in tandem, AthenH was convinced that the Nazis could acquire an advantage on the field.

So, AthenH appreciated the fair participation of the Luftwaffe in the battle and he proposed dwarfing the land infantry only to the needed strength.

AthenH of course, won the bid to execute his plan over Hitler's. His plans seemed promising to Hitler and to the other delegates. However, AthenH's motives were not rooted in brotherhood or for the betterment of the Nazi cause. Instead, he worked on his own political ambitions and secretly paved ways to achieve them - which no one except him were conscious of.

As the attacks commenced, it rained hell in France. The Luftwaffe terrorised the French cities, generously dropping love tokens from the sky as a return treat for what France had gifted them during WWI.

In the borders, the Nazi infantry strategically cut down and encircled the French military divisions inactivating French aggression at the front.

A few divisions marched into the cities cutting supplies and disarming the French troops. And, in a matter of few weeks, the Nazi forces were clear of further aggressions, and France was in Hitler's pockets.

The attack on France, choreographed by AthenH demonstrated the sheer potential of Blitzkrieg as a war model and AthenH's acumen.

During the French battle, AthenH in the background secured Hitler's authorization for increasing the manufacturing of aircraft dedicated to the forthcoming confrontation with Britain. AthenH also believed French airspace could be exploited to serve as a rehearsal ground to train the army for all the other genuine conflicts in the future. AthenH commanded and trained the air and land forces together establishing a coordination - unleashing a new way of war - and at every move transforming 'Blitzkrieg', to an even finer war model.

The momentous victory in France was enough to persuade Hitler to grant AthenH, a position on par with his. Hitler also viewed him as a prospective successor to the Nazi reign. Besides this, there was a mysterious personal connection Hitler had with AthenH for years.

Having France under their foot, AthenH, next targeted Britain. But he felt it was too quick to initiate another war. He believed the pace of aggression was a bit too fast, as he feared the world might perceive it as nothing but pure antagonism - a circumstance that AthenH genuinely wanted to avoid.

He suggested holding talks with Ostwald Mosley - a Fascist and antisemitic leader in Britain - who held the same ideals as the Nazi Party. He insisted on funding the British Union of Fascists led by Ostwald Mosley to raise their power internally in the country and win Britain through democratic elections. AthenH knew such a battle with Britain would bleed them white, and would end up being a war of attrition. A war of such fate, of course, didn't connect the dots with his own secret political ambitions.

However, Hitler and his entrenched order were in haste and this time the war was commanded by Hitler. The battle commenced with Nazis taking the clear lead. Even during the battle, AthenH attempted to convince Hitler - but it was almost impossible to persuade Hitler on this subject as Hitler himself never trusted third parties and formal alliances.

After several rounds of counsel, AthenH's perfectly tailored flattering skills finally triumphed, and AthenH was successful in diverting Hitler to his ways. AthenH was granted permission to engage in negotiations with Mosley.

Nevertheless, Hitler disagreed to abort the battle.

Despite the internal chaos that AthenH caused with the Nazi counsel, the German forces turned out to be completely unstoppable on the field. The same forces which battled France were put to play in Britain as well. The forces demonstrated their invincibility just as they had during Blitzkrieg in France. They shined - all thanks to AthenH.

The British forces were left scurrying for their lives, as the Nazi infantry unmercifully took down everything that came through the way. Soon, the battle reached its conclusion with Hitler assuming command and taking the lead.

By now, Hitler turned a bit complacent, and so did his forces. AthenH knew they'll win the first phases of battles, but he also very well recognized the formidable capabilities of the Royal Air Force of Britain - which was the main reason that convinced him to take a different route than Hitler.

Winston Churchill braced Britain for the forthcoming aerial combat - one that terrorised even the Luftwaffe. AthenH tried to talk Hitler out of it and reconsider the strategy, but the situation already reached a stage where no one could halt its course.

The Luftwaffe swirled in through the British air space initially assuming the lead. However, in a speck of a time, the Royal Air Force retaliated and started to hit back, intensifying the tension. Pilots from both sides flew in shifts without sleep - yet witnessing nightmares every waking moment.

As days passed, the traffic in the already defiled sky just kept increasing. The number of operational airmen dying peaked, but the supply of pilots seemed never-ending. This never-ending aerial rivalry never seemed to end - as AthenH had already forethought.

Converse to the fact that the battle's purpose was the projection of military strength, it in a way just bled both parties off resources. Even after several objections from AthenH, the Nazi delegates never relented, and failed to grasp the futility of the pointless aggression. Pride and ego blurred their sanity. But, after months of unwanted aggression, their resources were drained. Germany was forced to relent, and in the end, Britain emerged triumphant!

Amidst this long war, AthenH stealthy managed to tie hands with the British Union of Fascists and Ostwald Mosley. Through negotiations, AthenH managed to secure concessions regarding the British borders in exchange for Nazi membership and power to Ostwald Mosley. AthenH and Mosley became close and started working on same ideals.

The British citizens lost faith in Winston Churchill post the protracted war, despite their win. This shift of sentiment appeared to favour Ostwald Mosley, and he started garnering fame and popular support.

AthenH, meanwhile secretly began funding the antisemitic groups in Britain to work in his favour - but what exactly were his real motives?

3

The Accident

Adolf Hitler - the man who casted spells with his utterly polite speeches, the man who very humbly terrorised several races, the man who so generously offered death to millions, was also the man who cultivated a public image portraying himself as celibate. Strange enough, but not true!

Adolf Hitler, in his late thirties, had a romantic relationship with a young girl - Maria Reiter - while living in Bavaria. Maria was a shop worker and Hitler fell in love with

Maria as he would make frequent visits to the shop. As days went on, Hitler developed a lust for her and frequently forced her into sexual activities. Despite Maria having a strong dislike, they had several dates and spent a lot of time together. The relationship was half-built and secret. But who is to say accidents won't happen? And, it did. Hitler impregnated Maria - the details of which remained completely unspoken to their families.

Hitler knew such a matter, if disclosed, would be politically damaging to him as well as sabotage the 'huge political mission' he had vowed to achieve. So, Hitler left Maria Reiter and busied himself with his political career.

Maria gave birth to a baby boy, whom she refused to parent. In the later years, she enjoyed a personal marriage life, with all the secrets hidden. However, it wouldn't last. Her marriage life failed just a few years into it.

Following the dissolution of her marriage, she chose to live alone for the rest of her life. She neither cared about her partner nor the child she once gave birth to. But Hitler often found himself thinking of Maria - whom he never saw again.

Maria's child was raised in a foster home during his infancy but later was adopted by a couple residing in the countryside. He was named 'Freiheit' - freedom. While receiving care from his parents, they noticed how he showed remarkable political boldness and was very keen on political thoughts. He was bright, and his acumen surprised his parents and friends.

In his teenage years, he developed excessive interest towards the idea of 'democracy' and staunchly opposed Hitler's dictatorial regime. He began expressing his anger through his very controversial works that he drafted and harboured strong political hatred towards Hitler and his Nazi regime.

Days passed to months and months to years.

When Freiheit was old enough he started venturing on his own. He became aware of his childhood adoption and eventually discovered the true identity of his biological parents.

It was a profound and unexpected surprise to find about the mysterious relationship he shared with Adolf Hitler.

Anyone would rather have a happy feeling when they find themselves in such a situation.

But he was wise enough to set aside any sentiments and still resolutely stood against his own father and opposed the ideologies his father held.

Frehiet decided to change Germany's fate. He knew it was impractically and just mere stupidity to oppose Hitler's rule by protesting against him or through political opposition. So, he devised a different plan and decided to merge with the Nazi counsel and assume himself as a genuine delegate to work on his goals.

Frehiet created for himself an alias to be known by - 'AthenH'. His primary motives were to assist Hitler in occupying territories, and then betray him being his own son to establish a wide democracy over entire Europe - which not only would free Germany from plight, but also the other European nations.

4

The Bloodbath

While wounded Germany was recovering its arms and ammunition, and rebuilding its muscles after the defeat, AthenH was busy devoting his efforts to helping Mosley secure victory in the elections in Britain. Once again, his flattery proved its fineness as he was able to spellbind the entire counsel of the Union of Fascists, swaying them into his approach. Adolf Hitler himself was unaware of all the witty tactics that AthenH had been conducting to win Britain, but Hitler was sure of his man AthenH- very sure indeed!

AthenH believed winning Britain held a greater significance than conquering Soviet Russia. However, Hitler wouldn't wait. Unwilling to delay his plans, he boldly initiated 'Operation Barbarossa' - the code name for the invasion of Soviet Russia. Despite the horrific defeat in Britain, Hitler still maintained a complacent attitude that drove him into false convictions about his abilities, and he thought he could walk over Russia with ease. But undoubtingly that wouldn't be the case.

While Germany adopted Blitzkrieg, Russia adopted a war of production - they were quite confident about the ineffectiveness of Blitzkrieg on their soil. As AthenH was busy with his secret propaganda in Britain, Hitler decided to command Operation Barbarossa.

Invading Russia was not an easy challenge. The only pathway towards attacking Russia was from the west - but moving ahead through the west would render their military might a waste, as the entire land was covered in snow and in such cold temperatures it would be a nightmare to battle.

Additionally, aircraft and other modern arms would unquestionably serve no purpose as they can't be operated in such inhospitable conditions.

Nevertheless, the Nazis went ahead. The battle commenced as an inaugural treat for Hitler, as the Nazi troops advanced very well without Soviet resistance - but little did they know, it was a set trap.

Joseph Stalin, having been already aware of the challenges of engaging in direct warfare on the western front and well knew battling in the West would be a mishap as the climate would limit their military abilities. He also knew it would be impossible to defeat the Nazis head-on, at the front, so he wisely chose to employ dummies and decoys in order to deceive and ensnare the advancing Nazis on the western front. He chose to employ a war of production, as he knew the Western climate would slow down the Nazis. The Red Army deployed untrained soldiers, and prisoners to fight the Nazis at the Western Front.

Being unaware of the disguise, the Nazi troops advanced ahead.

Germans started registering stunning success - or at least according to them - as the panzers demolished everything they found in sight. The smaller Russian cities in the west gradually started falling for Hitler's very keen military plans - indeed everyone thought so!

Starting off from the border, city after city was sieged and taken control of. However, when they reached a certain point, the real aggression of the Red Army began. Stalin chose to hit back this time, as the decoys were now all down.

By this time, Mosley in Britain had won the parliamentary election with the assistance of AthenH. And now, Hitler passed on the command to AthenH.

AthenH, having silently hunted Britain, now rather wanted to lose with the Russians.

He, however, wanted to save the Nazi troops but was welcoming a grand defeat. And, who knows what he scripted for the future? It was time for Soviet Russia to experience the real thrill!

AthenH commanded the Wehrmacht to leverage its full might. The battlefield erupted in chaos. Heavy tanks rolling forward, their treads crushing everything in the way and leaving behind beautiful trails... The soldiers pushed their limits, manoeuvring the fields with guns with their tanned uniforms. While the aircraft painted the Soviet sky in great art of trailing smoke and flames. On the ground, the splashing red blood created patterns on the dark battlefield ground, and flags of different shades waved despite all the chaos. The whole battlefield seemed like a beautiful art being painted by the mortal soldiers - but it didn't last long.

AthenH then signalled his troops to attack cities, rather than combat the Red Army in their area of strength.

Hitler's war machine started to show its might again, projecting its evil and brawny way of war. The Russian cities were ruthlessly shelled - so intense, to the standard no one could ever conceive of. And it wasn't leaflets dropping this time - they had learnt enough from the English men already! Bombs rained down the sky, with sirens blaring at every inch of the country. However, the resistance was nothing less - the Soviet aircraft equally combatted the Luftwaffe, slowly taking down Hitler's hopes.

Soon, the Nazis were losing supplies in the field, and it took a long time to summon reinforcements. As the Nazi troops had advanced very far into the Russian land, it was hard for resupplies to arrive.

Capitalising on the lack of arms, slowly, the Red Army started taking the lead. It seemed like Stalin had foreseen the events, as he very well chose a war of production. And, now that

Russia had enough supplies of arms, tanks, aircraft and artillery, it sounded easy to beat the Swastika!

The Soviet hit back dealt huge damage to the German army, who had underestimated the Soviet military abilities. Stalin was impatient and mean - very much. He didn't even allow the smoke and dust to depart peacefully from the battlefield, as he, in no time, started his next round of attack.

He commanded the Red Army to crush the Nazi troops and to leave nothing, but just the metallic scent of blood in the field! The disarmed Nazi soldiers were hit hard, and they neither had command nor weapons to resist. The relentless assault launched by the Soviets seemed quicker than Blitzkrieg, giving the Nazis no time to even think, or even fear. Soon, their defences were reduced to rubbles.

Amidst this chaos, AthenH was patiently calculating how to map his dreams, while Hitler was trapped in a state of tension and unease. The Nazi troops in the field had to relent, as they were pushed to switch to the defensive. With it, Hitler was intensely humiliated.

The Red Army had showered a bloodbath on the Nazis!

5

The Comeback

When the entirety of Germany was sunk in humiliation due to the defeat, AthenH found the defeat promising, yet he wasn't content with its scale - he had expected something grand. However, Adolf Hitler for obvious reasons was in fantastic distress - the situation which AthenH found the most comfortable detailing his plans about. You know, flattery is sharpest when used against distress and anger! Hitler yearned to rebel back but had neither arms nor position.

AthenH then commanded the troops to remain dormant in Russia, until they were reinforced with soldiers and resupplied with arms. It was impossible to send reinforcements within days, it took weeks. And before they could even arrive, winter arrived. The Red Army had vacated major parts of the west before the snow came. However, the German troops found themselves with no alternative but to set their camps in the snow. Soon, the weather deteriorated, and the number of men being hospitalised due to frostbite outnumbered those who were wounded.

Until the resupplies could arrive, Operation Barbarossa was put to a halt.

In Britain, it was all glory. Mosley started strengthening his political presence and winning over the majority. The ultimate motive was to translate the garnered power to establish an authoritarian government along the lines of Nazi principles. The general public however was unaware of these plans, but Mosley was pretty confident about them.

While the Nazis were stabilising their positions, AthenH had already sketched his own master plan for his rise to power, or for the downfall of the Nazis. The plan was to permit the Russians to barge into Germany, let them assume the lead and deceive them into victory. However, a counterattack would be launched in Russia by the British troops - who shall be Nazi troops by the time of the attack - navigating through the Black Sea, while the Red Army shall be busy scouting the dead German land. The scheme drafted appeared convincing, but AthenH will have to orchestrate it perfectly. And, if done right, Europe would be his!

Now, the crux of the matter was the mighty Soviets. It took just a few weeks for Germany to repair itself from the damages, and the resupplies and extra men had reached Russia by this time. As that happened, AthenH also ordered Mosley to have the British military trained and prepared.

Joseph Stalin was unaware of Hitler's impending vengeance still hidden in the Soviet land - Stalin wasn't expecting any attacks. The Nazi delegates remained unsure whether to retaliate or relent, until the very last moment. Meanwhile, the German soldiers imposing penance upon themselves were waiting to rebel. They couldn't resist. The urge to decipher the enigmas, expecting an affirmation had them awake. It wasn't just dots and lines that they were waiting for. Those were the codes that inevitably were going to dictate the fate of two of greatest European powers of the time. And, they received it! Hitler affirmed the mission - well why wouldn't he?

Wehrmacht, all set, launched a surprise attack on Moscow by midnight. Moscow was bombed - important centres and the Kremlin. With it, AthenH backed the Nazi troops off the Soviet land.

It was groundbreaking, something that held remarkable interest, something that unquestionably had the whole world looking. This was all Hitler needed, but AthenH rather saw this as a trigger that would infuriate the Red Army further and would draw them into Germany. But until then, Hitler would be at the helm. Having hit the Kremlin, he was content with his doings for the first time ever and perhaps forever!

With his man AthenH stabilising the Nazi order, and Mosley operating in Britain, Hitler decided to break for a while. Amongst his busy war schedule, he often thinks about one - Eva Braun and his long-standing silent relationship with her. Eva Braun was initially introduced to Hitler as a personal photographer for one of his ministers. From then Hitler and Eva Braun have been in a close relationship for years. A few years into, they lived together but later broke apart due to Hitler's busy schedule. But they never forgot to remember each other. They often met for a quick talk, but Hitler's busy work never let them spend considerable time together.

Now that he assumed his political stand was at the peak, Hitler handed down the roles to AthenH and decided to break for a while with Eva Braun. Eva Braun wanted to marry him, but Hitler wouldn't consent - he thought it would be a disgrace to his political life and reputation. Besides, he was already 55!

Meanwhile, AthenH decided to pursue his goals silently while the Fuhrer was off. He held talks with pro-Nazi parties and Fascist organisations in Soviet Russia to help him drive the enraged Red Army into German land. AthenH funded them to organise local riots and movements which pressured Stalin. AthenH also sought the assistance of Mosley for this.

AthenH was doing all he could to forcefully infuriate the Russians into invading Berlin.

Taking down the Soviets, Hitler believed would unravel the utopian Nazi-led paradise he had long been envisioning. Conversely, AthenH believed it would be a key towards establish a larger and finer version of democracy which guarantees real peace.

With AthenH chairing the Nazi counsel, the fuse finally ignited!

6

The Reciprocal

The Red Army launched an unprovoked invasion on Germany!

It always seemed like Hitler shared an unbreakable connection with war and politics - a connection so deep that they could finish each other's sentences. It had been just days Hitler was off, and war summoned him back!

He was hastily called up at midnight, just to be informed about the Soviet breach into his land. Initially, Hitler couldn't believe it. He wouldn't.

Who would dare to encroach into the Nazi field? Or, at least dare to raise their flag against the Swastika? No bird would dare to challenge an eagle...

But now the eagle has unfortunately become a prisoner of false trust...

A caged eagle can well be within the reach of even a bear!

And, so would the bear come for the eagle. At midnight, the Soviets launched their attack into the German borders, grandiosely heralding its entry into a war that was to eventually dictate the fate of Europe. The invasion was a surprise to both Hitler and AthenH. However, their reactions were split. Fortunate for AthenH, and unfortunate for Hitler. That's how real surprises are!

Hitler and AthenH, sharing command, began the retaliation. Soldiers were commanded to seal the borders and the Luftwaffe was instructed to clear the air space of foreigners. It worked well on Hitler's end, but AthenH deliberately let the Red Army advance in.

By this point, Hitler lacked a cogent strategic plan to fight back the Soviets. However, AthenH had already drafted the act of war in his favour and had also outlined the plans for his future military campaigns.

The battle commenced with severe damage to the German land. However, in days, the Wehrmacht neutralised their position. Not only would this battle be the most horrific battle ever fought, but also the one that would ultimately conclude what Europe would mould into - a home for peaceful states or a living hell.

The battle shook Europe, and the fear it instilled, resonated throughout the globe.

The fierce struggle couldn't, and wouldn't promise life. Men died every other moment, not even having peaceful seconds to contemplate what they were fighting for or ponder whether part of a fight would really bring out true peace.

Men died, yearning for brotherhood and help. Men died, with tears rolling down - the tears carrying their hopes for the future. Men died, carrying the red flags - a few with golden hammers, and a few with Swastika.

Men died, not even knowing it was their own leaders who set apart their country's ideals from what the golden hammer and sickle signified - which in reality was a testimony of brotherhood. Men died, not even knowing that the Swastika symbolises divinity. Men died, not knowing their courage would reign for ages!

Men were fighting hoping their part would bring peace, but never knew the meaning of peace. Men died, not knowing how to choose peace... Men died, not knowing what is peace...

Rifles and bayonets clashed, as the valiant soldiers fought for securing every inch of the land. Tanks rumbled across the battlefield, their cannons firing with lethal force, leaving behind trails of destruction. The aircrafts were roaring through the sky, dropping some round bodies which after landing, blossomed into a mass of fire and vengeance. Explosions bloomed in the sky as missiles found their targets. Nights were still bright as days, with fireworks always there to illuminate the skies - not failing to threaten even the clouds.

The battle persisted for months with both sides holding neutral positions, until the Germans soon started running out of supplies. Russia had from the beginning adopted a war strategy focused on production, which of course helped them stay healthy throughout the battle. Meanwhile, the months of expenditure had bled the Nazis white. The German military started backing off steadily from the borders, it was time the Red Army went inland to gather some blood!

The Soviets finally had somehow invaded the Nazi territory, which seemed almost inconceivable just weeks back, owing to the magnitude with which the Nazis had retaliated to the Soviet attack. Adolf Hitler was pushed to stay on the defensive, and he found his bunker as a permanent residence.

The Nazi counsel was in chaos - except for AthenH though. Hitler felt a deep sense of betrayal by his fellows and was in utter pain. By now, AthenH well knew that end of Hitler's tyranny was imminent. So, he planned to escape.

Within days, Germany had lost control and the Nazi counsel was left with no choice but to surrender their lives. Hitler chose to be with Eva Braun in his last days. Despite the Nazi counsel losing hope, Hitler had it saved. However, all the hopes vanished when he learned that the Soviets were already approaching his bunker. In his last days, Hitler chose to marry Eva Braun - as she had wished from the very beginning.

Coming close to death, he ordered the burning of all records and traces in the bunker and distributed cyanide capsules to everyone. He also ordered the burning of his body after his death. As the Soviets closed in, Adolf Hitler - the man who terrorised millions and knew no fear himself, committed suicide.

It was the end of Adolf Hitler! After orchestrating a majestic political masterpiece, he left the world.

Destiny turned the tide for Hitler. But... where had AthenH been?

He was the tide, himself!

7

The Dawn

AthenH had escaped to Britain, where his fellow Mosley had set ready a fleet of soldiers and aircraft for him. In Germany, AthenH successfully destroyed all the minds which had been long wanting power, not to rule but to oppress.

In Germany, the capital had fallen into the hands of Stalin - or at least, that was it according to the Soviets and the world. Stalin had ordered the inspection of Germany to find traces and clues about the Nazis and Hitler. Stalin, along with his troops spent weeks carefully scouting the dead land. However, they wouldn't know that life was still lingering, waiting for someone to resurrect it back, stronger.

AthenH, back in Britain, forged the army, which was, after careful planning, transported to the south Soviet shore via the Black Sea using the English vessels.

It was a no deal for AthenH to pull Mosley onto his side. Well, AthenH does that with ease. When his flattery could win countries, why wouldn't it win a person.

As the major part of the Red Army and Stalin himself were busy scanning Berlin for traces, it was easy for AthenH's army to take command of Moscow.

Moscow was down.

Now, with AthenH commanding his fleet from the east, and Mosley commanding from Britain in the west, they encircled Stalin and his desperate troops from all sides. The Red Army surrendered.

AthenH chose the right form of peace, decimating what people thought was peace, under the tyranny of their not so peaceful leaders.

It was the dawn of a new era!

An era of true democracy. The era that assured the togetherness of every race despite its identity. An era of free speech and will. An era that embraced peace, law and order. A constitution was formed, and it would be called after Adolf Hitler - not for teaching them democracy and peace, but for teaching them how not to choose peace and democracy.

Freiheit was welcomed grandly by the people who had been for long the victims of fear and oppression.

Freiheit decided to preserve the identity of the Nazi party as he transitioned to democracy, a wider and well-established political system.

British colonies would be freed.   Europe would be his but by peoples will.

Europe would flourish under the peaceful governance of the Nazi leadership.

Swastika, now truly seemed to be the epitome of divinity. The eagle had become the dove, decimating the power by authority, and welcoming power by choice.

AthenH's Swastika flew high at its apogee - The Luftwaffe was the tyrant of the sky, the

Kriegsmarine diplomatically ruled the waves, and Wehrmacht, the land!

What next? The moon?

Peace

www.ingramcontent.com/pod-product-compliance
Lightning Source LLC
Chambersburg PA
CBHW061442160726
47995CB00003B/1003